LEAGUE OF THE
PARANORMAL

THE
GHOST
RUNNER

NORWYN MACTÍRE

DARBY CREEK
MINNEAPOLIS

Darby Creek
A division of Lerner Publishing Group, Inc.
241 First Avenue North
Minneapolis, MN 55401 USA

For reading levels and more information, look up this title at www.lernerbooks.com.

Image credits: Chris Bailey/Getty Images (sneakers); LoudRedCreative/Getty Images (texture); komkrit Preechachanwate/Shutterstock.com (texture); alexkava/Getty Images (shoe icon).

Main body text set in Janson Text LT Std 12/17.5.
Typeface provided by Adobe Systems

Library of Congress Cataloging-in-Publication Data

Names: MacTire, Norwyn, author.
Title: The Ghost Runner / Norwyn MacTire.
Description: Minneapolis : Darby Creek, [2019] | Series: League of the paranormal |
    Summary: High school senior Ollie discovers a ghost haunting a cross country track
    through the woods and, with his best friend and teammate, Nate, decides to lay it
    to rest.
Identifiers: LCCN 2018045943 (print) | LCCN 2018051955 (ebook) |
    ISBN 9781541556973 (eb pdf) | ISBN 9781541556812 (lb : alk. paper) |
    ISBN 9781541572959 (pb : alk. paper)
Subjects: | CYAC: Ghosts—Fiction. | Haunted places—Fiction. | Running—Fiction. |
    High schools—Fiction. | Schools—Fiction.
Classification: LCC PZ7.1.M25877 (ebook) | LCC PZ7.1.M25877 Gho 2019 (print) |
    DDC [Fic]—dc23

LC record available at https://lccn.loc.gov/2018045943

Manufactured in the United States of America
1-46115-43490-4/10/2019

1

Every season, Ollie Hernandez memorized
the back of Nate Dawson's racing spikes.
He knew Nate's shoes better than he knew
his own. Better than anybody else's. Within
a few races, Ollie's mind would capture
every detail.

Senior year's model had a white midsole on
top of a black outsole. A red heel with a white
logo in the center. Gold trim along the space
above that. A short white heel tab, one that
wouldn't wear on Nate's Achilles tendon. Nate
was careful about that, Ollie remembered—a
taller, aqua-colored heel tab had caused Nate
trouble in ninth grade.

Ollie did none of this remembering on purpose. It had more to do with circumstance. For three-plus years of Westlake High School cross-country, Ollie had run behind Nate. And close behind him too. Close enough to get a really good look at his teammate's footwear. Ollie had even won ribbons. Lots of second- and third-place ribbons. He was the next-best high school distance runner in the town of Westlake, Iowa. The next best in the county. Probably the next best in the state. But he had never beaten Nate Dawson.

Today a coating of mud covered the logo on Nate's heel. A rainstorm had come earlier in the day, a harsh one for October. The water had turned the course at Harding into a mud pit. But the order of the runners was the same as usual. Nate in first. Ollie in second. A few guys from the Harding High and St. Sebastian varsity teams behind them. Nate and Ollie's teammate, Carter Voss, at the back of that pack.

They darted past the second mile marker and the volunteers alongside it. Two miles into the five-kilometer race, with 1.1 miles to go. It looked like a win for Westlake High. But that's how a win becomes a loss, Coach Green would tell them. You decide the 5K is yours before you cross the finish line.

The Westlake High Whales had taken State in boys' and girls' cross-country three years in a row. That meant more than a dozen teams in the conference were chasing them. And, like Coach said, any one of them could grab Westlake's spot.

The mud got worse as Ollie ran on. With each stride, specks of wet earth flew upward, sticking to Ollie until they covered most of his lower half. The Harding course had seen three races that afternoon already—girls' varsity, boys' JV, and girls' JV. Ollie's sister, Luz, a junior, had placed first among the girls. She stood covered in a reflective blanket and shouted, "Move it, dude!" as Ollie passed the two-and-a-half-mile mark. Ollie grinned but kept his forward stare.

Nate was maybe a hundred meters ahead of Ollie, mud bursting around his shoes too.

Somewhere behind them was the rest of the pack. Close enough that Ollie could hear their feet hit the mud. Light little splashes like that gave each race its own rhythm. The sounds told him he had a good fifty meters before the next man.

His chest burned. That was fine. You had to like the burn a little bit to run this kind of race. Runners were weird that way.

He had time to pick up the pace. Not a lot of time, but maybe enough. This was the hard part—convincing himself that he could catch Nate, even pass him. That this race could be different, after years in second place.

He tried to pump his legs, to will himself toward a quicker pace, but he was starting to tighten up. Calves, quads, everything. This was what always happened. Wanting to catch Nate wasn't enough. Forget about gaining ground. At this stage of the race, holding on was its own challenge.

Ollie took the course's last turn, reaching the final straightaway before the finish line. Six hundred meters left at most. He felt himself tipping sideways at the turn's edge, his muddy feet ready to slip out from under him. He windmilled his arms, slowed down his strides, doing anything to maintain his footing. Coach Aymes, the Westlake High boys' assistant coach, met Ollie's eye. Unsympathetic.

"This is no time to fall apart, Hernandez!" the old man yelled. "Harding's on your back, you idler!"

Coach Aymes. A part of the program for decades, much longer than Coach Green. Outside of this part-time gig, he was retired. He'd once been the school librarian, people said, half-guessing. Few folks in Westlake would have been around long enough to say for sure. But despite his advanced age, Coach Aymes showed up at practice every autumn to help train the boys' squad. Mostly by calling them idlers.

He was the heart of the team, the guys would joke. The cold, dark heart.

Coaches, family, and runners from earlier races lined both sides of the Harding course's final straightaway. This was the good part, when the usual noises of the race went away. After fifteen minutes of nothing but the sound of footsteps and Ollie's own breath, cheers began to surround him. The open-air straightaway became a tunnel of noise, pushing Ollie forward. The tightness in his legs and the burning in his chest both went away. That part of the race was already over.

He watched Nate cross the finish line ahead of him. For the moment, even that was fine. With two hundred meters to go, Ollie felt free. He sprinted the last half minute, and the crowd's cheers turned into a roar. Done.

"There we go, Ollie!" Coach Green shouted. "Good race!"

Past the finish line, Ollie stumbled, trying to rest his hands on his knees but continuing to walk. If he stopped right then, he'd tighten up again, worse than before. Off the straightaway, the crowd noise no longer at its loudest, the sound of his breath reentered his ears. And that sounded pretty loud too. As a course official handed Ollie a heat blanket, he glanced back at the race. Guys from Harding,

St. Sebastian, and South Pleasant would finish next. After them, the next runner in a navy Whales top: Carter. None of them close to Nate and Ollie.

First-place Nate and second-place Ollie.

Being one of the first guys to finish meant coming back to a deserted athletic tent. All the JV guys would still be standing along the straightaway, rooting for the rest of the varsity squad. That was all right, Ollie thought. The way things were supposed to be. Some of the freshmen had even worked out a chant involving whale noises. Ollie could never recognize it during an actual race, but he appreciated the effort. Still, the minutes after a race were always strange. All that work, that final rush, and then—the quiet.

Ollie stood at the tent's edge, peeling off his dirt-caked racing spikes and wondering how he was going to slip his warm-up pants back on without making the insides of them completely muddy. He tiptoed around his teammates' bags, looking for his own. Once he reached it, he let himself sit for the first time since crossing the finish line. Stretching his hamstrings, enough to avoid a cramp.

He startled as a hand patted his shoulder. He looked up to see Nate, a huge grin on his face, holding out a bottle of something bright and green.

"What is that?"

"It's called ElectroLyft," Nate said. "I guess it helps you get your electrolytes back twice as fast as other sports drinks. They sell it at these, like, sports specialty stores. My mom bought a whole case. I brought some for both of us!"

Ollie popped off the bottle's black cap and took a sip. "It's . . . thick?"

"Yep," Nate said. "Kind of weird. But if you want one next week too, I have fourteen more back at home."

He took a sip of his own, winced, and then took a huge gulp anyway. He smiled and said, "By the way, great race. We crushed it, man. Was that a personal record for you?"

"Close," Ollie said.

"Nice. Anyway, yeah. You know how people say so many guys peak by, like, junior year or so? Not you, dude. I feel like you're only getting better. I noticed at practice the other day, too, when you . . ."

Second-place Ollie and first-place Nate. It wasn't how Ollie wanted people to think of him. But that wasn't Nate's fault. Nate Dawson was the best friend he'd ever had.

2

Ollie's locker was directly next to Carter Voss's. This was, at all times, a cruel and unfair situation. But it was the worst the day after a cross-country meet. The day after a cross-country meet, Carter would attempt to tell Ollie all the reasons why, really, Carter should have beaten both Ollie and Nate. Then Carter would explain why he was going to beat them the next time. This had never happened, but Carter seemed to believe every word of his trash talk. The whole thing would've been kind of sad, if Carter wasn't such a jerk.

Carter was an *enormous* jerk.

Ollie and his sister had arrived at Westlake High that morning with only a few minutes until first period. And maybe that was good timing, Ollie had thought, hustling from the parking lot to the main entrance. Maybe Carter had already stored his things, taken out what he needed, and walked to class. Maybe Ollie wouldn't have to talk with Carter at all.

But when he reached the hallway with the senior class's lockers, there was Carter. He stood next to his open locker, clipping his fingernails. No one else clipped their fingernails in the hallway. Ollie didn't even understand why a person would *want* to. But that was Carter, a loud and stupid young man.

Ollie stopped at the water fountain several feet from his own locker. Maybe, after a long drink, Carter would be gone. Just to hold off for even longer, Ollie filled up his water bottle next. But after clipping his fingernails, Carter had started to check something on his phone, not moving from his spot. With a minute or two left before precalc started, Ollie headed over and started to spin his dial lock.

"You got a lucky rabbit foot in there?" Carter asked.

"No," Ollie said. "Just textbooks."

"Next time, you're gonna need a whole lucky rabbit," Carter said.

"Okay, but right now I'm just going to get a textbook."

"Because I'm closing in on you," Carter continued. "You *and* Nate. Say good-bye to that buddy-system thing you've got going on, 'cause I'm about to bust through you guys. You two can fight for second. Only reason you beat me yesterday was I ate something weird. On the bus. Bad granola."

"Bad granola," Ollie said. "That one-hundred-percent checks out. Hey, I'm almost late for math. And chemistry is on the second floor, so you're definitely gonna be late."

He slid his precalc book into his bag, pushed the locker shut, and started down the hallway toward the math rooms. Carter's locker slammed shut behind him.

"Hey. Ollie. You know why I'm gonna beat Nate, and you never will?"

Ollie kept walking.

"You don't have that edge. I don't know if you settle for second best or if you just keep choking, but you don't have it. That's the difference between me and you. No killer instinct."

"You sound like a commercial," Ollie said before he turned a corner. "Not a good one."

He was late to precalc, but not by much. The teacher, Mrs. Ramos, raised an eyebrow as Ollie slipped into his seat, but she didn't say anything.

Don't have that edge. No killer instinct.

The morning's lesson was on complex numbers, which Ollie thought he understood, but Mrs. Ramos kept saying things that confused him. Maybe he just wasn't hearing her right. Carter's words wouldn't leave his head.

Don't have that edge. No killer instinct.

These were the kind of things people said when they were trying to sell you protein shakes or a gym membership. Just empty slogans that guys like Carter loved to repeat. But Ollie's brain kept playing them back.

Don't have that edge. No killer instinct.

What bothered him was, for the first time Ollie could remember, even if it was practically an accident, Carter might have been right.

* * *

Ollie and his sister had both been runners since middle school, but Luz hadn't become one of Westlake High's top athletes until the end of her sophomore season. She was an alternate at State that year, ended up having to run, and surprised everyone by coming in tenth overall. As a junior, she had become one of the best the school had seen in years. Ollie was proud, but the change had made things weird, at least at family dinner the day after a race.

When Luz was younger, she hardly seemed to notice that competition was a part of cross-country. She just liked to run. So their parents never felt awkward talking about how well Ollie had placed, even if Luz hadn't placed nearly as well. But now Luz was placing first in every meet of the season, and Ollie continued to come in second. So the conversation had changed. He could tell that, with each mention of Thursday's races, his parents were afraid they might hurt his feelings somehow.

Their mom had been working at the clinic during the away meet, but their dad had driven to Harding, and a day later, he was still giving her his account of the races. "That girl from South Pleasant—the tall one, McKinney—was leading for the first two miles, but Luz was smart, she drafted. And then poof, the McKinney girl tired herself out." He raised a shrimp to his mouth, then stopped. "And with Ollie, he was ahead of South Pleasant the whole time."

This was how the conversation went lately: *Hooray, Luz! Not that we forgot about you, Ollie.*

"I think our Luz is poised for first in State," their dad said.

"Pssh, you're gonna jinx it," Luz told him.

"And your whole team is in for another win, Ollie," their dad continued.

Ollie wanted to say, *Dad, it's fine.* But that would have meant talking about the whole issue, out loud, which would have been even more awkward. He was relieved when they started talking about a new movie coming out next week.

"Is this the one with the giant bird?" Luz asked.

"You're thinking of *LA Falcon*," Ollie said. "I think this one's about lava?"

Their dad grinned across the table at their mom. "What do you say? Is it a date?"

"I would see it if you wanted," she said. "I like the lead actor."

"I think she likes him a little *too* much," their dad said and winked at Luz.

"He seems like a nice man!" their mom said.

After dinner, Ollie washed the dishes and then, on the way to his room, stopped and knocked on Luz's door. Then he knocked again. This was the usual routine.

A minute or two later, Luz opened the door, plucked out her ear buds, and told him to come in. Ollie stepped over the turntable and mixing board she had lying on her floor and sat on the black exercise ball opposite Luz's computer chair.

"I have a question," he said, trying not to roll off the exercise ball.

"Sure."

"It's kind of weird," he told her.

"Weird is good. I like weird."

"What's it like," Ollie asked his sister, "to be the best? On your team, I mean."

Her face sank. "Oh," Luz said. "Oh, *buddy*."

"Don't, don't, don't," Ollie said, waving his hands in defense. "No pity. I just—I don't know. I guess I've just been thinking about it lately. Always losing to Nate. It'd be different if I was like the third-best guy on JV. Not so much pressure. But always coming in second in these varsity races—I don't know how to describe it. Maybe you wonder more about how it feels if you're always that close but never right at the top."

"Well," Luz said. "First is weird too. 'Cause there's nowhere to go, dude. I'm not complaining. But it's like—now what I gotta do is maintain. That's it?" She shook her head. "You're lucky. You've got a 'next thing' to think about."

"Doesn't feel that lucky. And I won't have a shot at the next thing for much longer. We've got two meets left. One is State, and then *bam*. Senior year cross-country's done."

Luz shrugged. "As the younger sibling, I reserve the right to not know the best advice for you. But Ollie, I tried starting a livestream account where I talk about running. And let me tell you: the internet does *not* care about cross-country. Everybody's losing at something."

"That's a happy thought."

3

"For the last eight weeks, you've represented this high school and the town of Westlake across the state of Iowa," Coach Green said. "Now the competition comes to us."

The man was an artist when it came to a pre-race speech, but the ones he gave during home meets could be downright epic.

"We've already qualified for State. I know it. You know it. And you deserve it. You've run strong races all year. But if I see anyone out there looking complacent, if I see anyone not out to give it his best, you better keep in mind that your spot in that championship meet is not a given. You earn it. Every race. Every time."

One week after the meet in Harding, Westlake High was racing on its home course, an arboretum next to the school. Mostly smooth, nice and green, but a few stretches could be brutal. In other words, it was a good place to train. The state championships would take place there too, a week and a half later.

The back-to-back home meets were the result of a weird schedule. The Whales had run almost a whole season without home-field advantage, but they were ending it on familiar ground. Assistant Coach Aymes had called it a fine way to conclude.

"You're out there today in front of your family, your friends," Coach Green continued. "Take it as a time to shine. You deserve that too."

Before the varsity runners took off their warm-ups, Coach Green asked Coach Aymes if he had anything to add.

"Only this," the older man began. "It is tempting to look beyond today to next week's grand finale. But as Coach Green so sensibly suggested, each race is a chance for the very best of us to emerge."

The varsity runners looked to one another, unsure of whether they were supposed to clap or whether Aymes had even finished. This was the usual effect of a pep talk from the assistant coach. The boys settled for some fist bumps and then ditched their warm-ups.

As they jogged to the starting line, Nate whispered to Ollie: "They really should stop ending the speeches with Coach Aymes."

Carter stuck his head between the two of them. "I think Coach Green knows I what I know. It's time to shine. I'm coming for your spot, Nate."

"Well, I hope your tummy's okay," Ollie said flatly.

Carter jogged ahead of them and grinned over his shoulder. "Just try not to choke, Ollie. It'll keep me from getting bored out there."

At the starting line, the runners arranged themselves while a pair of volunteers took off in a golf cart. Westlake High used the cart to make sure runners in the lead made the correct turns. It was a courtesy for visiting teams, at least in theory. People joked that Westlake

High wouldn't need the course cart as long as Nate Dawson was part of a race.

"No edge, man," Carter whispered to Ollie. "None of that killer instinct."

Ollie said nothing.

And with a loud pop, they were off.

To the left of the navy blue Whales squad was St. Sebastian, its runners clad in maroon uniforms. To the right was Chambers City High in canary yellow. Races always began with these masses of color, and then the usual formations started to appear. The orange of Harding High started to mix with St. Sebastian's maroon in the corner of Ollie's eye. A pair of runners in Millertown green weaved in front of him. Those guys started strong, but they would get tired. They always did.

And Nate was in the lead.

Ollie liked this about Nate. He always had. Since they were freshmen, Nate would take the lead early—no messing around.

He could hear Carter behind him too. A certain person's footsteps were hard to identify, at least with this many runners around. But he knew the sound of Carter's breathing—somehow louder than everybody else's.

And so Ollie pushed ahead. Away from Carter and then beyond the runners from Millertown. Passing guys until he had his usual view of Nate's shoes. And then he heard Carter again. Not behind him but in his head.

Don't have that edge. No killer instinct.

And Ollie kept pushing. He wanted to know what first felt like.

As they reached the marker for mile one, he overtook Nate, grabbing the lead. The volunteer watching from the passenger's seat of the course cart looked very surprised.

"All right!" Nate huffed. "We got this!"

That proved one thing at least, Ollie thought. Nate could get passed and still be the nicest dude on the team.

For the next half mile, Ollie felt more or less the same as he usually did after getting one-third of the way through the course. The pace was intense, but nothing he hadn't trained for. The late October air was crisp but not cold and filled his lungs gently. Whatever extra strain he might be taking on, he had extra drive too. And he knew that a few paces behind him, Nate had to be smiling a bit.

They came upon a stretch of open ground among the arboretum's clusters of trees. Ollie's dad was there on the other side of the course's white line, standing with some other Westlake parents and shouting, "Woo-hoo!"

Nearer to the end of the second mile, Ollie's body could tell that it had not been running Ollie's usual race. Some alarm bells began to go off. He knew each sensation— the burning in his chest, the tightness in his legs, the dryness on his tongue. But they were coming on too soon. Way too soon.

For the next twenty or thirty seconds, he kept ahead of Nate, but a hill was coming up next, and no one did hills better than Nate Dawson. Ollie wouldn't be *giving up* his lead, he thought. More like, it was just inevitable that he would *lose* it. A given. The hill was where Nate would pass him.

But was that why Ollie always came in second? Taking something like that as a given?

He chanced a look behind him. Nobody from one of the other schools was anywhere nearby. But Nate was even closer than Ollie had thought.

"Let's own this!" Nate huffed. "Doin' great!"

They took the first strides of the hill side by side. Nate wheezed encouragement. Ollie couldn't speak at all. The burn intensified, Ollie's limbs feeling twice as heavy as they'd been on level ground. At the top of the hill, a familiar sight came into view. The back of Nate's spikes again.

"Come on, Ollz!" Nate shouted. How could he shout right then? "Keep with me!"

As the ground flattened out again, Ollie watched Nate's heels getting farther in front of him, the course cart maybe fifty meters ahead of Nate. All of them were headed for the Skyless Trail.

On a really hot day, the Skyless Trail was like a length of heaven. Tall red oak trees formed walls along a wide grass pathway, their branches so large and so many that they blocked out much of the sun. That day, with Ollie losing any chance of a first-place finish, entering the trail was like entering five hundred meters of gloom. For the next couple minutes, he'd be alone, watching Nate shrink, before coming out onto the home stretch in his usual, predictable position.

But then Ollie saw Nate shift sideways, his head turned to the woods alongside them. Nate tried to keep running, but in a way unlike him. His strides were sloppy, zig-zagging down the path. As if Nate had been startled, but not by anything Ollie could see. And then Ollie heard something he'd never heard before: Nate screamed. He began what looked like an all-out sprint before tumbling forward and collapsing on the grass.

"Nate!" Ollie shouted, his voice returning to him. He reached Nate a minute or so later. His friend lay sprawled on the ground. Hyperventilating, his face white. Cradling his left leg.

"My ankle," Nate said. "Ollie, keep going! Please, Ollie!, You have to finish. Just don't look at the woods—"

A gnarled root stuck out of the ground nearby. After Nate had spun out, he must have tripped. It would be another five minutes, easy, before the medical cart at the back of the race reached them, so Ollie shouted for the cart in front to turn around. Nate's left ankle was bent, his shin and foot forming a sideways *L*.

The course cart stopped near the trail exit, the riders appearing to hear Ollie's shouts. The two volunteers looked to each other, maybe unsure of when they were allowed to turn around.

Ollie cried out again—"He's hurt!"—and the golf cart began reversing toward them. As it approached, the sound of thundering footsteps began to grow. Runners in orange, yellow, maroon, heading down the Skyless Trail.

"Ollie, you gotta finish," Nate said. "I'm fine—don't—"

"It's all right, man," Ollie said, helping Nate onto his good foot as the men from the cart rushed over. "It's all right."

Ollie watched the flock of uniforms come by. Part of him wanted to follow—there was still time for him to catch up—but the other part knew he should stay and help his friend. He watched after the runners in uncertainty.

"Ollie, *go*," Nate said, attempting a faint smile. "Come on."

By then the herd of runners had passed them, exiting the trail and beginning the course's final five hundred or so meters. Ollie started forward again, but slowly. Tentative. He was already sore from stopping and confused about what could have spooked Nate. He turned back once more and spotted another group of runners, Carter among them, and began to get himself in gear.

During Ollie's final strides down the Skyless Trail, he allowed himself one more look back. He could see Nate, stretched out along the back seat of the golf cart. Carter, passing the cart with wide eyes. And among the trees nearest Nate, another figure, tall and white. Faceless—no, not faceless, but with features Ollie couldn't recognize. Somewhat like a person, somewhat like something else. Like the skull of a wolf or an elk hung across its face. Its blank eyes, its mouth, seemed to vibrate, unwilling to stay in one place. It turned its head from Nate toward Ollie. Ollie's blood ran cold.

4

Ollie placed eighth overall that day, with
Carter close behind him in eleventh place.
Westlake High boys' varsity scored outside
a meet's top five teams for the first time in
years. It was a good thing they had already
qualified for State. Nate texted Ollie from the
hospital that night to tell him that his ankle
was broken.

On the day of the race, Coach Green had
been too distracted by Nate's injury to truly
chew out the rest of varsity. But at Friday's
practice, he made the time.

"That was the *exact opposite* of what we
wanted to happen," he told the team. "When

one of us goes down, the rest of you need to step up."

The team sat stretching on a practice field while Coach Green held court.

"Now, I've talked to Nate's mother, and he'll be out the rest of the season. We're going to pass around a card for all of you to sign, and I encourage you to give him all your best wishes. But this is an excuse for absolutely none of you to start taking it easy."

Joe Peng, one of the team's freshmen, was smart mouthed but a good kid. One of the guys who created the whale-sound cheer. A little sheepishly, he raised his hand. "Should the course maybe not have that part in the Skyless Trail? Like, since a guy got hurt?"

"If you'll allow me, Coach Green," said Assistant Coach Aymes. "Every course has its hazards. Regrettable, but it's true. And the oaks are so thick around the path that I see no clear alternative. But more importantly, the Skyless Trail is part of our tradition. And tradition is the lifeblood of this program."

Emphasis on the blood, Ollie thought, rolling

his eyes. Overly dramatic speeches about tradition were typical with Coach Aymes.

Before the team began its usual day-after-a-race workout, a slow five-mile run, the coaches pulled Ollie aside.

"I expect you to be up front today," Coach Green said. "You're the top runner on this team now. We've got State in eight days. For the next week, I need you to lead."

Coach Aymes added: "I must agree. As of yesterday, there is no better competitor on this team."

The honor didn't fit Ollie the way he'd thought it would. Like a shirt that was scratchy and too tight. Like it belonged to somebody else.

* * *

Ollie visited Nate the first chance he could get, which was late Saturday morning. Nate's mother let him in politely but absentmindedly. It was just the two of them in the house. Nate's dad had left when Nate was a sixth grader. Nate didn't often talk about that. He preferred cheerful subjects. But Ollie knew that for Nate's mom, her son was the most important thing in the world. Sometimes Nate felt way too fussed-over as a result. He didn't mind complaining to Ollie about it. Ollie could only imagine what the last two days had been like for them.

Ollie closed the front door behind him once it was clear Nate's mom would have left it swinging open. When he caught up to her, she was surveying Nate and his bedroom. Already protective of her son, she seemed to act as if he might break his other ankle any second, even as he rested in his room. Once she confirmed there was no new cause for concern, she left Nate and Ollie alone.

Nate was sitting up in his bed, a brace around his foot, sipping orange juice through a straw.

"My mom insists," he said, putting his glass down. "On some level she probably knows that OJ doesn't fix a broken ankle, but I think tending to me—constantly—makes her feel better about the situation."

Ollie took a seat on the old, patched-up easy chair sitting in the corner of Nate's room. "How does it feel?"

"The ankle? Not so bad, if I avoid putting pressure on it. I mean, long-distance guy equals weird high pain tolerance and stuff. But it could be worse."

"I'm sorry, man."

"That's all right," Nate said. "Let's talk about you. Congratulations. You're gonna be leading the Whales at State."

"It's not the way I would have wanted it," Ollie said. "And you're still the better runner. You got us there."

"Well, right now, I'm not exactly a runner at all. And you're gonna be great, Ollie. I wish it could be the two of us out there next week, getting that last state championship. But if that's not the way it is, you're gonna be great."

"Man," Ollie laughed, "I don't know how you got to be so good while still being so nice."

"Well, cross-country's weird that way. I don't think I'd last long as an ultimate fighter."

Ollie laughed, then shifted from sitting in

the easy chair to half leaning on Nate's desk. He was having trouble staying still.

"So what . . ." Ollie started, "what happened?"

He had told himself before the visit that he wouldn't mention what he'd seen at the edge of the woods. More importantly, he had told himself that he *hadn't* seen what he thought he had seen. It was like this: Ollie had been running the hardest 5K of his life. He'd been fatigued and shocked for his friend too. That could give you visions. Apparently. He still didn't know what had made Nate flip out. But Nate would have an explanation for that.

For the first time since Ollie entered the bedroom, Nate's expression fell. "What do you mean?"

"Back in the Skyless Trail," Ollie said. "I mean, I know you ran into that root, but—"

"Yeah," Nate said. He fiddled with the straw in his glass. "Tripped over the root."

"Right. But before that—"

"I don't know why I didn't see it there," Nate said. "We've run that course a million times."

"So was there anything, though, that—"

A sucking sound interrupted Ollie: Nate's straw at the bottom of his now empty glass.

"Could you do me a favor?" Nate asked him suddenly. "Could you find my mom, maybe ask her if I can get some more of this? I know I complained about it, but it's actually really good juice."

Ollie narrowed his brows. "Sure."

"After that, I'm probably gonna get some more rest."

"Right, for sure," Ollie told him. "You gotta heal up."

He took the glass from Nate and closed the bedroom door behind him. This was fine. If Nate didn't remember much from before he tripped, this was fine. A lot had happened at once. It was a huge bummer that Nate was hurt, but the guy seemed to feel okay about it, and he even seemed happy for Ollie. Of course he did. Nate was the best. He'd get Nate some more orange juice, like Nate wanted. All of this was fine.

5

In the days before the state meet, practice was nowhere near as grueling as it had been at the beginning of the season. For one thing, Ollie and his teammates were in peak condition now. For another, Coach Green didn't want to risk anyone else getting injured. On Monday, they ran on the Westlake High track, doing an interval workout. Tuesday was a six-mile road run, but at an easier pace than usual. Nothing severe. The practices were just about people maintaining the shape they were in. But the atmosphere was tense.

Ollie blamed himself for some of that. He wasn't the natural captain that Nate had been.

He was quieter, less likely to think of the right compliment at the right time. Before last week, he hadn't needed to. He also hadn't realized just how much Nate's energy linked the varsity squad together. Without Nate, it was like the group had no center. No voice. Unless Ollie counted Carter, who filled most pauses with trash talk.

After the previous week's race, all the guys on junior varsity were done for the season. Only ten guys continued to attend practice. Seven of them would go on to compete at State, and three would be alternates. In addition to Ollie and Carter, the practice squad included three more seniors, Duncan Perry, Aaden Akoom, and Kyle Schwartz; three juniors, Malcolm Wong, Reed Bryan, and Geoff Hansen; and two sophomores, Santiago Cruz and Scott Leonard. They'd been running together in one combination or another all season, but the week so far had felt like an extended icebreaker game.

"Nice work," Ollie had told Scott and Santi after Tuesday's long run. The two of them said

thanks like they were doing him a favor. Or
was that in Ollie's head? Nate probably never
had those kinds of doubts. That's what made
Nate who he was. A leader.

Wednesday's practice brought the squad
back to the arboretum. They'd do a light run
through the course and then a series of sprints,
to work on finishing. After Coach Green
explained the workout, Ollie glanced around
the stretching circle. He looked for concern,
even just curiosity, on people's faces. But when
no one else reacted, he said, "Does that include
the Skyless Trail?"

Coach Green said nothing for a moment,
then asked Ollie, "Will that be a problem for
you, Hernandez?"

This time, Ollie's teammates took notice.
Each one looked up to see what he'd say next.
"No," Ollie said. "No sir."

On the jog over to the course, Coach
Green asked Ollie to hold back. "You all right,
Hernandez?"

Ollie nodded.

"I know you and Dawson are close. And

I know you're taking his injury hard. But now is not the time for you to lose your nerve," Coach Green said. "We're running the course because it's the same course we're running on Saturday. No other team has that privilege. And that means we run *all* of it. Understand?"

Ollie nodded again. He'd run the trail. They all would. And that would be fine.

Carter started the Wednesday run in front. Ollie let him. Being captain didn't mean being at the literal front of the pack at every practice. This was how people got hurt, he reminded himself. Went too hard at practice when they didn't need to, pulled something or burned themselves out.

Well, it was *one* way they got hurt.

As the group reached the course's big hill, a chill ran through Ollie. Not a kind he'd ever felt before. Not race-time adrenaline coming on during practice. Not a cold-weather-run feeling either. For an Iowa fall, the temperature was mild, low sixties. This was pure apprehension. Soon they'd begin the Skyless Trail.

Carter had remained at the start of the

pack, with Aaden, Reed, and Malcolm at his heels. Ollie hung close behind them. Carter could lead, but an unwritten rule said that Ollie, as the new team captain, couldn't fall too far toward the back. He passed Malcolm at the top of the hill, and Carter shouted, "About time we see some hustle from you!"

The Skyless Trail was at least ten degrees cooler than the length of the course before it. Chills came over Ollie again. Maybe it *was* just the temperature, he thought.

A couple minutes later, they were approaching the root that had messed up Nate's ankle. It rose from the ground—in plain sight, Ollie noticed, even in the dimness of the trail. Hard to miss it, unless you were—

"Watch out, boys!" Carter shouted. "There's a Dawson trap up ahead!"

Here too, Ollie wasn't sure what to say. Carter wanted conflict. That was obvious. And he *definitely* wanted attention. But teammates weren't supposed to make fun of a season-ending injury either. Nate would have known what to do, if he hadn't been the one injured.

Ollie peeked behind him, to see if the rest of the squad had heard Carter. And then he saw it again. At the edge of the woods. Lean and white. Its body fading in and out of view.

And this time Ollie screamed. "Guys! Guys—run!"

But instead, they slowed down, staring at Ollie.

"We kind of are, dude," Reed said.

Ollie pointed toward the pale figure as he shuffled away from it. "Look! *Look!*"

Malcolm had caught up to Ollie and stopped beside him, squinting toward the woods. "What am I looking for?"

Ollie pushed him forward. "Malcolm, no! Run! Go!"

The figure remained at the edge of the woods, motionless except for the opening of its mouth, a slow, inhuman unfolding.

Soon, it said, its strange voice echoing in Ollie's head. *Soon.*

Ollie's shuddering intensified, the temperature around him continuing to drop.

"Now!" he shouted. "We have to go!"

Ollie sprinted the rest of the trail, past Carter, Aaden, and Reed, who had all stopped to watch him. Once the sunlight hit him, Ollie looked backward, gasping, seeing nothing but his teammates and the oak trees. He stopped for a second, his head spinning, and then began to run again. More than he wanted confirmation of what he'd seen, he wanted to get away from the trail.

He didn't get far. Fifty meters from the far end of the Skyless Trail, Coach Green and Coach Aymes stood with their arms folded. He could tell by their faces that they'd heard everything.

6

"I don't know what that was," Coach Green said. "But if you're too shaken up to compete at State, you need to tell me right now."

"A complete disruption," Coach Aymes said. "Unacceptable."

If Ollie told them he had spotted something in the forest, *described* it, his season was over. No doubt about it. Even the varsity guys he would have counted on to back him up didn't seem to have seen or heard a thing.

And he'd worked too hard to take himself out of the race. Freshman year, sophomore year, junior year, and now senior year. Even with Nate out, Westlake High still had a shot at the state championship. And Ollie had a shot at best in the state. He couldn't give that up. He wasn't even sure about what he had witnessed. The only thing he was certain of was that he couldn't let himself get sidelined. For him and for Nate, he had to race.

"I'm—I'm okay," Ollie said. "I'll be better tomorrow. One hundred percent. I think maybe I didn't drink enough water . . ."

Coach Green raised an eyebrow, clearly not convinced.

". . . And Carter was making jokes about Nate. It—it got to me."

Coach Green didn't comment right away, but he lowered his eyebrow again. That part must have made more sense.

"Then be better tomorrow. You're a leader now, Ollie. Still a leader. But I need focus."

Ollie thanked the coaches and jogged back to the Westlake High parking lot alone. He didn't know how he'd feel on Thursday. He couldn't think ahead even one day yet. First, he needed to talk to Nate.

* * *

Ollie ate his post-practice dinner fast. Faster than his mom would have liked, he could tell. But when he explained that he had plans to meet Nate afterward, she understood.

"How's he doing, anyway?" Ollie's dad asked.

"He's all right," Ollie said. "You know, it sucks. But he's Nate. He has a better attitude about it than most people would. When I saw him on Saturday, he was doing fine."

For the first ninety percent of the visit.

He drove over to Nate's, not sure what he would say. But he was sure he needed to say more. About it—whatever he had seen. What *they* had seen. Could he assume that much?

He had texted Nate first, asking to talk, but he didn't say why. He hadn't waited on a reply either. Nate's mom looked surprised when she saw Ollie at the door but invited him in and offered him one of the wellness smoothies she'd been blending. He told her he'd just eaten and asked if he could step into Nate's room.

Nate greeted Ollie with a cautious "What's up?" Cautious not because he was unsure about Ollie's intentions but because he clearly knew why Ollie had come.

Ollie closed the door behind him.

"I want to talk about the thing in the woods," he said. "Along the Skyless Trail."

Nate said nothing.

"You saw it, Nate, right? The day you tripped and broke your ankle."

Nate sighed. "I saw something. I don't know what. Not anything I'd seen before."

"I did too. Last week and then again today. This almost see-through thing. All glowing. It had a—not a horse face, but it didn't look like a person either. And these eyes, like—I dunno, black holes or something."

Nate nodded.

"Well?"

"Well *what*, Ollie?" It was a tone he'd never heard in Nate's voice. Nate liked to face a challenge head-on. But he'd never faced anything like this.

"What do you think it is?"

"It could be a prank," Nate said. "Probably? Right? Kids from one of the other schools, trying to psych us out."

"Yeah," Ollie said. "But like—with nobody seeing them enter or leave the woods around the trail? At some point, someone would've spotted a group of kids dragging a giant ghost-thing back to their car. And I saw it at practice today, Nate. No one's coming back to Westlake a week later to pull the same prank *again*, when there's not even a race happening."

"I know, I know," Nate said. "But—all right, what if it's not another school? What if it's someone like Carter?"

"That would be easier, I guess. He'd know a good place to do a prank like that. He's got a few friends, somehow, who could help. It helps explain the practice part. And he was talking the other day about killer instinct. Having an edge on people."

"There you go," Nate said. "I don't know how we'd bust him now, but—"

"Did it *feel* like a prank, though?" Ollie asked him. "Honestly."

Nate went silent again. He reached for his smoothie glass, empty.

"Come on, man, it's me," Ollie said. "And

whatever it is, I've seen it too. I'm asking: did it feel like a prank to you?"

"No."

"No," Ollie said. "Not for me either."

"But it has to be," Nate said. "No other explanation."

"None?"

Nate shook his head.

One of them had to say it. Ollie had wanted it to be Nate. But that wasn't happening. "What if it's a ghost or something?"

"I don't—" Nate started. "I don't think—" And he stopped again.

"I don't like the idea either," Ollie said. "But this time there were people right near me. The other guys training for State. I *pointed at* the thing. No one else saw it."

"It's not a ghost. Because there *aren't* ghosts."

Ollie couldn't remember the last time the two of them had argued, but he was learning quickly that he didn't have much patience for it. Trash talk from someone like Carter never felt good. But deflections from your best friend felt worse.

"All right," Ollie said. "If it's a prank or something, there's gotta be evidence, right? Footprints. Scraps of the disappearing papier-mâché monster. The bottle someone peed in while he was waiting for us to run down the trail."

"Probably, yeah," Nate said.

"Then I'll go find some."

"Ollie, wait," Nate said. "Forget it. The damage is done. Can we both forget it?"

"I'll be fine," Ollie said. "It'll be ten at night by the time I get out there. No one else from school's gonna be around. And you've ruled out ghosts, remember?"

Nate sat up in bed. "You're being an—"

Ollie quietly shut the door to Nate's bedroom and stepped back into the hallway. After this, he'd make a quick stop at home. Then on toward the Westlake Arboretum and the Skyless Trail. Toward the last place on Earth he wanted to be.

7

Ollie had parked the car on his family's street rather than in the garage. That way, his parents would be less likely to notice when he headed back out again. Once he was inside the house, he realized he hadn't even needed that kind of caution. His mom and dad were already asleep. Must have been a long few days. It certainly had been for Ollie.

His next stop was Luz's room. He knocked softly, not wanting to wake up his parents. No answer. He knocked again, still cautious. But if she had headphones on, there was a chance he'd be softly knocking all night.

When he texted Luz instead, she appeared

in her doorway a second later.

"Hey bro," she said. "What do you need?"

"Um, actually . . . your phone?"

The camera on Luz's phone was about ten times better than the camera on his. Which had never been an issue until Ollie needed to potentially take some nighttime shots in the middle of an already dark, wooded enclosure.

At first Luz asked for something to hold onto in return, then realized she didn't want to keep track of Ollie's phone in exchange or have his letter jacket taking up space in her room or take the key to his bike lock and lock his bike to itself.

"But don't you dare read my texts," she said. "If I get it back and you've opened any, your phone and the jacket *and* your bike are gonna be out on the lawn with a big cardboard sign that says *Free*."

"Fair enough," Ollie said.

"What do you need it for, anyway?"

"I'll know that when I see it."

* * *

Ollie approached the Westlake Arboretum with Luz's flashlight app on, but he kept the phone pointed at the ground. If anyone else was in the woods near the trail, the beam of light might tell them Ollie was coming. But he knew the course well enough to make his way inward just by looking at the ground.

In Ollie's other hand, he held his winter coat. The temperature had already dropped since practice. It was in the forties now. But Ollie didn't yet feel the kind of chill he had felt earlier. He hoped he wouldn't, hoped the coat would remain an item that he hadn't needed to bring.

As he got closer to the Skyless Trail, he was tempted again and again to stop and turn around. He hoped at least that Nate was right, even if Nate's refusal to consider anything except a prank had Ollie fuming earlier that night. And at the edge of the woods around the trail, he breathed a sigh of relief.

Shoe treads along the ground. Recent. They wouldn't have been from someone running one of the team's workouts, either.

The footprints clearly led off the trailhead and into the trees.

Before following the treads, Ollie snapped a photo of them. He couldn't try to play detective until later. No way to figure out who might be the owner of the shoes just yet. But he had his first bit of evidence now. That was huge. And if the footprints meant that a real, flesh-and-blood human was behind all this, even better. Ollie could write off the alternative: something stranger, unnatural. He wondered for a second how he'd let himself believe it at all.

With the photo taken, Ollie took his first step into the woods. He knew this ground less well, but even so, he kept the beam of the flashlight app low to the grass. If whoever was responsible were still nearby, Ollie would want to keep a safe distance. He was not about to throw an elbow at somebody two-and-a-half days before State. Evidence would have to be enough.

After five or so minutes of walking, Ollie stopped, suspecting that he had heard a voice or voices. Then, after keeping still for a minute or two longer, he was sure of it. He took his next few strides as if moving in slow motion, careful not to break any twigs or bump into branches. He even pulled on the winter coat, not needing it but worried it would snag on something otherwise.

One voice grew more familiar as Ollie approached. Not that Ollie could believe it. He stopped walking—stopped moving at all, too stunned for a moment. Then he turned off the app and pocketed the phone. Lowering himself to his knees, he peered over the top of a bush in front of him.

Deep within one of the Skyless Trail's wooded borders stood Assistant Coach Aymes, in his Westlake High Whales windbreaker. A soft white glow covered his face. The source of the glow stood opposite Coach Aymes: the pale figure. A chill descended upon Ollie once again.

Although he couldn't make out their words, he could tell Aymes spoke to the figure with a level of comfort. The old man did not seem to fear the thing, and he definitely did not seem to doubt its existence. Ollie continued to watch as Aymes knelt, stretching his arms out before the thin white being. The figure, in turn, touched its palms together and then raised its arms to the air. The glow around the thing intensified, swirling above both it and Aymes. The figure brought its arms down just as fast, sending the glow toward Aymes's chest.

The old man fell backward as if struck by lightning, motionless for a moment. And then Aymes rose again, saying: "Thank you, thank you, thank you!"

Shivering now, Ollie remembered why he'd come. He patted his pocket for Luz's phone. Even if only Aymes showed up in the photo, that would still be one cross-country coach caught sneaking around the course close to midnight, for reasons he would have to explain to Coach Green and the rest of the team. Withdrawing the phone, Ollie reached for its volume controls. He wanted to double check that he had the sound at zero before attempting his photo.

And his hand, shaking, pushed the volume up by mistake.

The phone buzzed first, then announced itself with a loud ping.

Aymes and the figure both turned in Ollie's direction. And Ollie ran. Ran between trees, leapt over bushes, ran like he'd never run before. The chill got worse, like ice was lining Ollie's chest, but he pumped his arms and didn't look back. Too panicked to even scream, he ran.

He sensed a presence behind him. Couldn't hear its steps but didn't have to. It was on his heels and in his head. The same word as before echoed in his ears: *Soon*.

Sometime after the phone had pinged— seconds, minutes, he wasn't sure—he had left the woods and found himself back on the Skyless Trail. He kept running as the chill threatened to overtake him. He hopped over the root that had taken down Nate and kept running. And then he was out, finished with the trail, onto the last stretch of the course. The presence was no longer behind him, and the night sky was clear above him.

He looked back, feeling it was safe to do that now. He saw nothing. The chill was gone as well—Ollie dripped with sweat all of a sudden. He yanked off his winter coat to see that the back of it had been ripped open. Exposed stuffing fell out onto the grass. Not the kind of evidence he'd hoped for.

As Ollie ran toward his parents' car, thoughts raced through his mind. Two kept circling back around.

The pale figure—whatever its name, its nature, its origins—was real. Ollie had to believe that now.

But that wasn't the scariest part.

He'd had a head start. Without one, the thing would have smoked him.

8

Later that night, Ollie hid his shredded coat in his family's garage. He buried it in a milk crate, folded underneath a bowling ball and a bike pump. Upstairs, he emailed himself the photo of Coach Aymes's footprint and then slid Luz's phone under her door.

Sleep seemed impossible, but he felt exhausted too. His body ached after his sprint out of the Skyless Trail. And so Ollie put himself to bed, burying himself under his comforter, making the heavy sheet part of a lie he tried to tell himself: that he was safe.

Whenever his eyelids fell, he saw the pale figure or Coach Aymes. Had Aymes seen *him*?

he wondered. If Aymes had, would the old man let on at Thursday's practice? Whatever else was true, neither he nor Ollie was supposed to be out near the cross-country course deep into the night. It might be a shared secret, Ollie thought, sealed by mutual distrust.

He was still sleepless by morning. He looked in the bathroom mirror to see his eyes had turned red, dark circles around them. In the same way his head had begged for sleep but refused it, Ollie's stomach growled and then rejected what he gave it. Eggs, veggie links, dry toast—nothing would stay down. He purposely missed the bus, pretending not to hear Luz's warnings. If he passed out on the way to school, Coach Green would definitely hear about it. If he kept himself on two feet, he could trust himself to stay that way. So he walked the mile and a half to Westlake High.

Ollie was late to first period, and his precalc teacher wasn't feeling so forgiving this time. Mrs. Ramos informed him after class that his repeated tardiness would be reflected in the behavior portion of his grade.

Second-period English managed to be worse. Ollie had forgotten completely that they were supposed to write an essay on the book they'd finished in class last week.

His stomach settled itself by lunchtime. Before the period ended, he even went up for a second chickpea salad, skipping his study hall afterward to eat it in the school courtyard. But his body had burned through the food by the time cross-country practice came around. He approached the stretching circle like a boy about to collapse. If Coach Aymes noticed— and had noticed Ollie the night before—the old man didn't let on.

The Thursday workout was an easy one, thankfully: a two-team relay race, with each team passing a filled water balloon from one runner to the next and starting over if its balloon burst. Coach Green had designed it to help the guys blow off steam two days before the state championship. Ollie managed to make his exhaustion look more like caution as he cupped the red balloon in his hands and passed it off four hundred meters later. Coach

Green was keeping an eye on him, he could tell, but the man never told Ollie to get in gear or stop messing around. Coach Aymes said nothing to Ollie either.

After the game, Coach Green and Coach Aymes gathered the varsity squad together.

"Listen up, Whales," Coach Green said. "We've had a great season so far. A setback last week, but I see you looking strong and looking focused. This Saturday, for your next state championship, all you need to do is run your race. That doesn't mean it'll be easy. But it's what you train for and it's what you know. We do it every week. And we *are* the best team in this state."

Aaden shouted, "Woo-hoo!" and just for a moment, Coach Green grinned.

"Now," Green continued, "it's my pleasure to announce our final lineup for State. As alternates, we'll have Bryan, Hansen, and Perry. Thank you, gentlemen, for coming with us."

The three boys nodded.

"And competing will be: Cruz. Leonard.

Wong. Akoom. Schwartz. Voss. And, as your team captain, Oliver Hernandez."

Aaden patted Ollie on the back, and Ollie patted him in return. He shared a smile with the sophomores too, as if to say *you're in*. Scott and Santi smiled back.

"I'll expect to see all of you in your warm-ups, at the course, at eight a.m. on Saturday," Coach Green said. "But before that, I'll see everybody at my house tomorrow night for the spaghetti dinner. Bring your appetites, because we're about to carbo-load. Now, everybody, on the count of three . . . One, two, three—"

"*Whales!*"

As Ollie's teammates dispersed, Coach Green asked Ollie to hang around for a second.

"I know I've been tough on you this week," Green said. "But that's only because I believe in you. And I can see the stress you've been putting on yourself."

Ollie nodded, relieved to let a little more of the stress show, knowing that some of it had been showing already and Coach hadn't decided to bench him.

"What I said back there about running your race, that goes for you especially, Ollie. For four years, you've been one of our best. And one of our most *consistent*. This is your chance to be first in the state. I can see how that might scare you a little. Fear's a killer like that. But this is the thing: all you've got to do is what you've been doing already. Like I say, it ain't easy. But it *is* simple. Just remember how good you are."

Ollie thanked Coach Green, meaning it, and believing the man's words too. With Nate hurt, he was the uncrowned best in all of Iowa. On Saturday, it was time to reach for the crown.

"I'll see you at dinner tomorrow," Coach Green said, but before Ollie could walk away, Coach Aymes's cracked face appeared between them.

"Oh, you can be on your way, Coach," Aymes said. "I have a small measure of wisdom I like to impart on all our captains before the state race. My own personal tradition."

9

"How are you feeling, Oliver?" asked Aymes. "Well rested?"

Coach Green had headed for his car, leaving Ollie alone with the assistant coach. Wind shook the fencing surrounding the track, and the sun began to set.

"I've been keeping my usual hours," Ollie said. "You?"

"Ha. You're clever, Ollie. I like that. You've never shined quite as brightly as your friend Nathan, but you're a clever boy. And so I thought we might speak for a moment."

"About?"

"About what has taken place," Aymes said.

"And what's to come. You're one of the chosen few now, Ollie. Do you understand what I mean?"

"If you've got a weird speech planned," Ollie said, "could you just get to it?"

"Very well. I'm sure you've heard it said many times this week that you're the best runner Westlake has to offer. But you may not yet appreciate what that means." Aymes rubbed his hands together. If he had any concerns about Ollie seeing him the night before, he still seemed to be enjoying himself. "You're aware that Nathan saw our pale friend? And then you did. Only the chosen can see it. And once seen, it can't be unseen."

"What *is* it?" Ollie asked, impatient already but unwilling to leave without answers.

"The Wraith of the Races," Aymes said. "That's how I used to describe it. The last boy it took called it the Ghost Runner. More modern, I suppose. But there's nothing I could say that would capture it completely. It's too old, too strange for any alphabet of ours."

"But why Nate? And why me?"

"Well—and this part, I'm afraid, is unavoidable—the Ghost Runner feeds on the energy of youth. It has for . . . longer than recorded history, I'm sure. One of you young lads every year. But—and please don't discount this, Oliver—it has a reasonably sporting disposition. Each autumn, it seeks out the very best our small corner of the world has to offer. That's why it moved from Nate, with his broken ankle, to you. It really does want the best. And then it races them down that wooded trail. Which, in more recent history, has doubled as a part of Westlake High's cross-country course. The races have always happened in some form, but organized sports make this *so much* easier to arrange. When the Ghost wins, it feasts on the life force of its opponent."

"And if the athlete wins he, what, *lives*?"

"I assume that's what would happen, yes. If I'm being honest, Oliver, I've only ever seen the Ghost come out ahead."

"How many times is that?" Ollie asked.

"Oh, it must be past two hundred now," Coach Aymes said. "I first came to Iowa around the turn of the nineteenth century. I had recently departed New York at the time. Wanted on charges of . . . well, I'll be honest with you, Oliver, it was quite a long list. And so I joined a caravan of French Canadians, off to mine the land here. The charges never did catch up with me, but the mining? Dreary work. Very soon, I was in need of an alternative. That, Oliver, is when I met the Ghost. It must have seen something in me. And—although I was never much of a runner myself—it let itself be seen.

"Since then, I've served as the Ghost Runner's eyes and ears beyond the woods," Aymes continued. "Always seeking out the next competitor. And as of late, I've ensured that the woods remain a part of the course as well. In return, by the good graces of my 'employer,' I've been able to enjoy another few centuries. I don't want to die either, Oliver. You see? We're alike in that, really. Both just making our way in the world."

Ollie stumbled backward. "You're— a lunatic."

"Then I'm a two-hundred-and-fifty-year-old lunatic," Aymes said, smiling wide, revealing a set of mangled teeth. "I must be doing something right."

"You're lying," Ollie said. "About some of this. You have to be. A missing boy—a missing *runner*—the *best* runner—every year? People would notice. They'd see a pattern. It'd be a whole crisis!"

"Please, Oliver," Aymes said. "We're talking about dark magic. Immortal spirits. Spreading a little collective amnesia throughout this town of hayseeds . . . For the Ghost, that's half the fun." Aymes smiled wider. "Let me ask you: do you know the name Paul Foley? Malik Marshall? Kirby Watson?"

Ollie shook his head.

"The fastest runners on the Westlake High School boys' cross-country team your freshman, sophomore, and junior year. It's funny. 'Second-place Ollie'—I hear the boys talk. And I know it makes you bristle. But really, they're being generous. They just don't know it. As a freshman, Nate was always second after Paul. As a sophomore, he was trailing Malik. Your junior year, it was Nate after Kirby. And you, Oliver? You were always third. At best."

The winds around them grew harsher, rattling the fence.

"It's not all bad," Aymes said. "Kirby, last year's boy. He loses, vanishes, and what do you know? His parents, separated a year before that, rekindle their marriage. Suddenly they have more time for each—"

Ollie spat in Aymes's face. "I refuse. I may be the best, but that doesn't mean I have to race. If your ghost sticks to the woods, guess what? I'm not going near them. I'll quit the team first."

"Hmm," Aymes said, wiping his cheek. "Another boy tried that, about ten years back. James Fitz was his name. Very willful. But this is one duty of mine. He had two younger siblings, this boy. Twins." Coach Aymes coughed. "I had a little conversation with James about his choices and how the consequences might . . . affect his siblings.

After that, this bold boy felt compelled to compete after all. It had to take place off-season, a little later in November. But we had our race. Everyone comes around. What's your sister's name, by the way? Luz?"

Ollie began to shake, his feet trembling in his shoes. He tried to speak again and couldn't find his voice at first. "Why—why are you telling me all this?"

"The first reason is the most obvious," Coach Aymes said. "No one will believe you. Even those who've lost a brother, a son— they've forgotten. That's how it works. But also—as I said, my benefactor is an oddly sporting thing. With that 'soon' business, for instance, the early glimpses of itself that it gives you . . . All a bit theatrical for my tastes, but it wants you to know what's coming. I imagine it thinks that's only fair."

With that, Coach Aymes began to shuffle away. He turned back briefly to say: "I'll see you on Saturday, Oliver. No spaghetti dinner for me, never cared for the stuff. And do rest up. The Ghost wants your best performance."

10

When Ollie reached home that night, the smell
of stuffed peppers baking in the oven hit him
from the doorway. His mother stepped out
of the kitchen to say, "I know you've got your
spaghetti dinner tomorrow, so tonight we're
making your favorite! Take a seat at the table.
They're almost ready."

As Ollie grabbed a chair, his father walked
into the dining room, stirring a large bowl.
"And lentil salad for Luz, my special recipe!
Only the finest for our two future champions."

"Thanks," Ollie said faintly.

As they all ate, Ollie struggled to listen to
the conversation around him. His dad talking

about the best spot at the arboretum for cheering runners, then teasing his mom about her Hollywood crushes again. Luz groaning. His mom changing the topic to the rush of patients they'd had at the clinic that day. Understaffed, all the time.

Ollie only heard stray words about any of it. His head felt light, the lack of sleep pulling at him again. But the peppers tasted amazing—they always did—with rice and cheese spilling out after his first bites.

"Thanks for dinner," Ollie told his parents again, forgetting he'd said it a few minutes earlier. "Mom, Dad—you know I love you? Right? That I appreciate everything you've—"

"Aw, Ollie, tonight's not about us!" his dad laughed. "We know, we know, but we're celebrating the two of you today. Now, Luz told us her squad earlier, but who from the boys' team's gonna be running at State?"

He could write them a good-bye note, he thought. Maybe it would disappear when Ollie did. Would vanish along with every trace of his name. Would empty out of his room along with everything else of his, every sign of his time on Earth. But he could try it anyway, hide the note somewhere. What else could a person do?

After dinner, Ollie's dad had refused to let him do that night's dishes, and Ollie said thanks once more, hugging both his parents. Next, he stopped at Luz's room. She opened the door at Ollie's first knock.

"Hey," she said. "Sup?"

Ollie held onto one side of Luz's doorway, in case dizziness set in.

"Um, not much," he said. "I—I just wanted you to know that I'm proud of you. Not just for the running stuff. You're awesome there, but I'm proud you're . . . such a cool person. And somebody I can count on. It's great, you know? And, um, never let anybody—"

"Dude, you sound like Dad," she said, laughing. "That's sweet, but I'm good, you know? I've got my game face on and everything. Or I know where to find it, anyway."

"All right, well, thanks, Luz. Love you."

She folded her arms, looking at him closely. "Is everything okay, Ollie?"

"Yeah," he sighed. "Yeah."

"Okay. Well, uh, love you too."

Ollie slept that night. Off and on. A couple hours at a stretch in the deep sleep of exhaustion, only to wake when the sight of the Ghost Runner's face entered his dreams. Until the last time, the last dream. He didn't startle awake, not right away. The Ghost's face grew larger and closer, its skinless skull the same size as Ollie's body, and then larger still. One of the ghost's vacant eyes stretched large enough to swallow Ollie. It covered him up, then dropped him on the grounds of the Skyless Trail. He ran to the finish, sweating, breathless, and found himself at the start again.

* * *

Ollie arrived at Coach Green's house that Friday evening after a school day full of looks from teachers who had grown less and less patient. The start-and-stop sleeping had continued through Ollie's morning classes. His only comfort was that he hadn't woken with a scream at any point.

Before he walked around to Coach's backyard, where Coach Green and a couple of parent volunteers would be serving up pasta from industrial-sized pots, he heard someone call from behind him, "Hey, Ollz! Help me to the back?"

Nate was exiting his mom's car on a pair of crutches. Ollie helped him assure her that he could assist Nate toward the backyard, and once she agreed, he offered to drive Nate home after the dinner too.

As he helped Nate up the first step, Ollie asked, "How's the ankle?"

"It's all right. I won't get another X-ray for a few more weeks, but at least my mom let me out of the house."

They took another step. Ollie nodded.

"Are you mad?" Nate asked.

"Nah," Ollie said. "Are you?"

"No," Nate said. He paused at the next step, staring at Ollie cautiously. "You look tired, man. You really went back there, didn't you?"

"Yeah."

"And?"

"We've got to talk," Ollie told Nate as he unlatched the backyard gate. "Later. I've got updates. Big ones."

Sitting at Coach's wooden outdoor table, swirling overcooked spaghetti around his fork was like drifting in between two worlds. One was familiar. Comfortable. Ollie even managed to laugh at Malcolm Wong's story about the time a goose chased him during a training run. The other world was uncertain. And unkind. A place where whole lives were forgotten, and people didn't have a choice.

Any time Ollie looked at Carter—and Coach wasn't also watching—Carter mouthed the words *tomorrow* and *you're done*. And once again, by accident, Carter was right.

After the team had finished carbo-loading, Coach Green told them again all they'd need to do on Saturday was run their race. That they would take the championship because they were the best and that's what they did.

But those other wins, Ollie thought, didn't

happen the way Coach remembered them.

He and Nate headed from Coach's house to Ollie's car, with Ollie popping open the passenger-side door and dropping Nate's crutches in the back seat. As soon as they'd both shut their doors again, Nate asked, "Well? What'd you find out?" And then, with a kind of desperate hope, "It was Carter, right?"

Ollie took out his phone and pulled up the photo he'd sent himself two nights earlier. "I found these. You see the footprints?"

"Whose? Voss's?"

Ollie shook his head. "Aymes."

"*What?*" Nate asked. "Are you *sure*?"

"I saw him. In the woods."

"But why would he—"

"He wasn't alone, Nate. The thing we saw—that I *know* you saw—it was with him."

Nate pushed the passenger door back open, then reached toward the back seat for one of his crutches. He pulled the crutch halfway onto his lap and dropped it again, deciding to ease himself out of the car first, a blur of panicked movements.

"That ride home? I'm good," he said. "I'll call my mom—I'll just ask if—"

"*Nate*," Ollie said. "Just let me ask you. Do I have any—*any*—reason to lie to you?"

Nate stopped moving. "No," he whispered.

And then Ollie told him everything. The two of them sat parked in the car outside Coach Green's house, and Ollie explained it all. Afterward, on the drive to Nate's house, neither of them spoke. But at the end of the ride, Nate looked over at Ollie, his face bright.

"I refuse to forget you, man," he said.

"I'm not sure you'll have a choice," Ollie told him.

"No," Nate said. "I think you can beat it."

"Nate—you've always been the nicest dude I know," Ollie said. "But on Wednesday, in the woods, the thing chased me. It's not human-fast. It's faster than that. I don't *want* to race it, but if they might hurt Luz, or you, or my folks . . . I have to."

"Yeah," Nate said. "I know. But I think you can beat it. Long-distance guy. Weird high pain tolerance. Remember?"

11

Saturday morning. The runners bunched together along the starting line. Then came the big pop. People rushing forward. The wide arrangement of athletes narrowing into something more like a line. Some guys paired up. Some tried to draft other runners. A few guys from Chambers City and Harding were near the lead, with Millertown ahead of them. All of it felt the same and yet completely different from every other race Ollie had run.

The first two miles of the race would be a gift. They demanded enough focus, enough hard work moment to moment, that Ollie's mind could only be ninety-five percent

fixed on the Ghost Runner waiting for him
later on. He hung with a guy from Harding
High, Wilberski, who had a similar first-mile
pace. The tiredness that had dogged Ollie
for the last couple of days disappeared. The
adrenaline—that was another gift at the start
of a race.

Ahead, Nate watched him from the back
of the course cart. Nate had been allowed
to ride in it for the boys' race. As long as he
didn't shout advice to other Westlake runners,
anyway. Any inappropriate cheering would
result in the disqualification of the guy on the
receiving end. But despite Nate's silence, his
eyes were expectant, intense. The adrenaline
had hit him too.

Mile one went by quickly. Ollie's family
stood near the mile marker, waving and hooting.

"Five-oh-five!" Ollie's dad called out.
"Beautiful first mile!"

"You got this, bro!" Luz hollered, her
Whales warm-ups back on and a first-place
medal around her neck.

A minute or two after that, Ollie made

space between himself and Wilberski. The guys from Millertown were still in the lead, but Ollie was closing the gap. And then he was midway through mile two. Another few minutes and he'd reach the Skyless Trail.

The first signs of the burn developed in Ollie's chest, and soon his legs felt tighter than they had at the beginning. Nothing he couldn't handle. Someone on the sidelines shouted, "Yeah, Carter!" So Carter must have been close behind him. Backing up the trash talk, almost. Up ahead, Nate gave Ollie a *What can you do?* expression.

The course's toughest hill, the lead-in to the Skyless Trail, was coming up. Assistant Coach Aymes stood at the bottom of it. Upon spotting Ollie, he cupped his hands to his mouth.

"Best of luck, Oliver." And then, grinning: "See you on the other side."

At the start of the hill, Ollie pulled even with the two runners from Millertown. Not pushing ahead of them yet. Waiting to see if one of the guys was the type to go really hard on the hill. It could be a trap, sometimes, trying to match another runner's pace at the wrong moment. But the hill had the opposite effect on them. Ollie passed the Millertown boys with maybe thirty meters to go before the Skyless Trail.

Ollie Hernandez, in the lead. He took a second to breathe deeply. Intentionally. To enjoy the moment as best he could, before the trail closed in around him.

He felt the cold first. Then the sunlight disappeared. Ollie was done with the hill, breathing harder than ever. In the dimness ahead, the course cart drove onward, and Nate shouted from the back of it.

"You can do this, Ollie! Just like we talked about!"

If the cart's other volunteers took their jobs seriously, this outburst from Nate would mean a disqualification for Ollie. It didn't matter. With his first steps onto the Skyless Trail, the real race would begin.

In a gleam of white light, the Ghost Runner appeared alongside Ollie. Much colder now, Ollie began to notice numbness in his fingers. He saw his breath dance ahead of him. And in the corner of his eye, he watched the figure pump its stringy, inhuman limbs. The race was on.

This close to the Ghost Runner, Ollie could hear it breathing, or whatever breathing-like-thing the ghost did. A sound like a bear at the bottom of a well, distant but undeniably powerful.

The two of them were neck-and-neck. Ollie running like he never had before. Begging his body to keep up the pace. It had to be this way.

It had to be convincing.

"Stay together, Ollie!" Nate shouted somewhere ahead of them. "Let's nail this thing!"

Twin sensations stabbed at Ollie, the burn in his chest and the unnatural coldness of the trail. He strained to keep near the Ghost Runner, but it moved one stride ahead.

This must have been what it felt like. For all the other boys. To run the race of your life. To try harder than you ever had before. And to know that you couldn't win.

The Skyless Trail grew darker as Ollie passed its midpoint, as if, beyond the treetops, the sky itself had turned black. Ahead of Ollie, the Ghost only got faster. Glowing faintly, it was the one thing Ollie could see clearly. Its clawed feet touched the ground, one and then the other, one and then the other, with no obvious impact. Lighter than air, like mist in the shape of a monster. A force no one could hope to outrace. Not alone.

"You're coming up on it, Ollie!" Nate cried. "Ten meters ahead, two meters to your right!"

Ollie winced and kept running. There was no avoiding what would come next.

And then he screamed. A scream not of fear but of pain. Unbelievable pain.

He fell on his side, clutching one leg, next to the large, gnarled root near the side of the trail. His ankle had shattered. Ollie was no longer able to run. No longer able to even walk. In no condition to compete at all.

"I did it, Nate!" Ollie wailed at the cart ahead. "*Man* does this hurt!"

The Ghost Runner whipped around, halting its forward strides, tilting its head. Despite the figure's strange features, Ollie knew the look: confusion.

"Hey, come have a look at this!" Ollie shouted at the ghost. "Does it look broken to you?"

The course cart had stopped at Ollie's scream, and Nate grabbed his crutches and stepped onto the grass, despite the cart's driver telling him to hang back.

"How bad is it?" Nate said, addressing the Ghost Runner this time. "Is he done for the season?"

The ghost turned its glare to Nate and back to Ollie. Its breaths were shorter, frustrated. It twisted toward the ankle Ollie had wrecked, unfolding its mouth as it leaned down.

Not by chance but by will, it said.

Ollie shrugged at the ghost. "I felt like someone else deserved a shot. Though *ugh*, I wish it wasn't Carter."

At that moment, Carter Voss darted past them, a look of horror crossing his face. He saw everything Ollie and Nate could see—including the tall, pale, glowing, unrecognizable Wraith of the Races.

"You'd better go get him," Ollie said to the Ghost Runner. "He's our top guy."

But by then Carter was meters ahead. Sprinting away from the scene of the accident, passing the course cart next. At the far end of the Skyless Trail.

The Ghost Runner bellowed with rage, taking off after Carter. Gaining on the boy, with fearsome speed. And an instant later, releasing its own howl of pain. Stopping, writhing, its body flickering in and out of sight more and more quickly. Until the body began to pull apart in a dozen different directions. Each of the ghost's limbs turned into separate clusters of countless points of light. The Ghost Runner, there and then gone.

Carter had made it out of the trail.

Carter Voss, the best runner in Westlake from the moment Ollie's ankle had broken, had outrun the Ghost Runner.

With the benefit of a slight head start.

12

In the rush to aid Ollie, the course cart volunteers forgot all about his and Nate's rule violation. Ollie avoided a disqualification. It didn't matter. In the final record of the boys' state championship race, he would go down as unable to finish. No points scored for Westlake High School from Oliver Hernandez.

But that didn't matter much either.

The Ghost Runner seemed to be gone. Off to wherever ghosts went when they died. Ollie couldn't be sure that the figure was gone for good, but it had certainly looked more like a full-on disappearance than just the ghost throwing a tantrum.

In spite of Ollie's injury, the Westlake Whales won their fourth state championship in four years. His broken ankle hadn't doomed the team. The scoring of the event counted a team's first five runners, not the full seven. So even with one man down, the Whales had enough points for the win. In fact, the sophomores, Scott and Santi, had really stepped up, passing a dozen other runners down the course's home stretch.

Carter, of course, was the hero of the day. He had taken first place overall and set a personal best too. After crossing the finish line, he had kept running, toward the Westlake High team tent, scrambling to find his warm-up clothes. If he had ruined his shorts at some point late in the competition, his teammates passed no judgment. Sometimes elite runners lost control of that sort of thing during a really intense race.

Once all the day's competitors had finished, the two runners who had started the season in the Westlake High's first and second spots rode toward the finish line. Each one sat in the back seat of a golf cart. For Nate, that meant the course cart, and for Ollie, the medical cart that had pulled up the rear.

Coach Green, soaked in a purple sports drink that the boys had dumped on him a few minutes earlier, dashed toward the carts as they neared the Westlake tent.

"Ollie, what happened!?" Coach shouted.

"Well, Coach, I know tradition's a big deal," Ollie said, "but you might want to change the layout of that course."

"I'm so sorry, kid," Coach Green said. "Next time I see Aymes, I'm telling him we've got to . . . Where *is* Coach Aymes?"

Green, Nate, and Ollie all scanned the area nearby. Coach Aymes was nowhere in sight.

* * *

In the weeks after the state championship, Ollie would sometimes dream of the Ghost Runner. He'd find himself back in the arboretum, no idea how he got there. And the ghost, resentful, would demand another race. Would howl and threaten him. Would turn the whole course, all of Westlake, into a freezing, skyless place. But then Ollie would wake up. Shivering and startled. But also sure that he'd find the figure nowhere but in his dreams. Maybe *that* was where ghosts went when they died.

That December, Ollie arrived home from school one day to see a thin brown package on the family doorstep. It arrived around this time every year. Inside the packing paper was a spiral-bound book that some parent volunteers put together, updating it annually. Its pages detailed the history of the Westlake High School boys' cross-country team. As freshmen and sophomores, Ollie and Nate would comb through every page, looking at the different rosters and records—times to beat, particularly good years.

He turned to Luz before entering their house. "Can you do me a favor? Can you actually take me to Nate's place?"

She sighed. Luz had driving duties on lockdown until Ollie's leg was back at one hundred perfect. "Fine. But you're finding your own ride home. Ever since I won State, I've been getting way more views on my running-tips livestream, and I said I'd be on at five."

Nate was already paging through the newest volume when Ollie rang his doorbell.

"It's a little weird, right?" Nate asked him. "Knowing what we know."

The page for their junior year listed Nate as a team captain and state champion, with Ollie in second behind him. The page for their sophomore year did the same. Repeating lies that the Ghost Runner had made all of Westlake believe.

"I wondered a few times about reaching out to some of the parents," Ollie said. "But it would probably just scare them. Like, some kid they don't know comes to their house, says they had a son but they don't remember him. I thought maybe, when we beat that thing, all that forgetting would've . . . I dunno. Come undone." He opened up his own volume of the cross-country annual, flipping to the stats about their freshman season. "I guess it didn't."

Nate nodded.

"But I've got a couple pens in my bag," Ollie said.

He handed one to Nate, turned to a blank page at the back of the annual, and began to write:

Paul Foley
Malik Marshall
Kirby Watson
James Fitz

Ollie looked at the names and wished he knew more of them. Wished there was some record, a way of knowing. And he knew there never would be.

But sometimes he would dream of other things. A band of runners two hundred strong, a warm autumn sun above them. Laughing, some of them. Swift but unhurried, out to feel the wind around them and the grass beneath their feet. After years of darkness, they had found the sky, and never again would it leave their sight.

ABOUT THE AUTHOR

Norwyn MacTíre is a writer—and an occasional runner—from Minneapolis.

LEAGUE OF THE PARANORMAL

THE
GHOST RUNNER

THE PARANORMAL PLAYBOOK

THE ROOKIE TRAP

THE TEAM CURSE

THERE'S MORE THAN JUST TEAM
SUPERSTITION AT PLAY HERE.